I0669712

Pamela A. Colman

The Lu Lu Alphabet

Pamela A. Colman

The Lu Lu Alphabet

ISBN/EAN: 9783337084370

Printed in Europe, USA, Canada, Australia, Japan

Cover: Foto ©Andreas Hilbeck / pixelio.de

More available books at **www.hansebooks.com**

For children small, both one and all,
    This little book is made ;
And if it teach as well as please,
    I shall be well repaid.

THE LU LU

ALPHABET.

NEW YORK:
HOWE & FERRY, 76 BOWERY.
1867.

A a

Stands for Alice,
So graceful and fair.

B b

For her Bridal,
And we were all there.

C c

For us Children,
As gay as e'er seen.

D d

The fine Dance
We had on the green.

E e

For Eliza,
Who joined us at that.

F f

The gay Feather
She wore in her hat.

G g

For the Grapes,
Much better than wine.

H h

For the Harp
Alice played on 'Lang syne.'

I i

For the Image
That stood in the hall.

J j

Is young James,
Who played with us all.

K k

For the Kite,
With colors so gay.

L l

For the Lady
In costly array.

M m

For the Melon,
Brought in by a friend.

N n

The bright Nosegay
The bridegroom did send.

O o

For the Oranges,
Delicious and sweet.

P p

For young Patty,
So cheerful and neat

Q q

For the Quinces,
All set in a row,

R r

The large Raspberries;
O! what a show!

S s

**For the Slipper,
One held in her hand.**

T t

The great Trumpet,
That sounded so grand.

U u

For my Uncle,
Who blew the loud blast

V v

The grand Villa,
In which this all passed.

W w

The Watch,
That dear Alice wore.

X x

For king Xerxes,
Who now lives no more.

Y y

For our Yeoman,
And with him did come,

Z z

The good Zebra,
To bring us all home.